Masai Ma

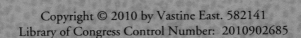

This book was printed in the United States of America.

To order additional copies of this book, contact:
Xlibris LLC
1-888-795-4274
www.Xlibris.com
Orders@Xlibris.com

Special thanks go to Lorena Birk for the breathtaking illustrations.

Masai Man

Predator or prey is the way of life on the East African Serengeti. I should know. I am a hyena, both predator and prey. I am the scavenger, the coward, and the laughing clown of the Serengeti. I am predator when the lion, called "King of the Beasts," is *not around. I am the prey when we cross paths. Sometimes the lion will pursue a different prey. On such an occasion I secretly witnessed from the tall brown brush of the Serengeti, a lone, frightened and skinny young boy struggling with fear, face the terror of the Serengeti. This is that boy's story.*

One rainy afternoon, with herds of grazing zebras, antelopes, and bouncing impalas off in the distance, a rather young boy, with his face painted bright-red and his hair in colorful red braids, followed four mumbling elderly tribesmen.

Walking in single file, they looked like an army of ants. After they reached a certain clearing away from the tall brush, their mumbling stopped. The chief elder at the front of the line turned and looked to the end of the line and beckoned the young boy to come forward. The young boy with gazelle-like legs ran quickly up to the chief elder.

"This is the spear of your father, take it!" said the chief tribal elder. His voice sounded like the rumbling thunder that chased the lightning across the rain-filled East African sky. "You must stay strong and be as brave as the lion; remember your brother, Tingdy," he added.

Tingdy slowly took the spear from the chief tribal elder and sheepishly said, "I will not fail you, Immopo."

Immopo sternly looked down at Tingdy. "It is not me you must not fail. You must not fail yourself. Remember your brother, Tingdy. Do you want to live in shame like your brother who failed to become a man by running wounded from a lion?" Tingdy could see Immopo's piercing black eyes floating on his rain-splattered, dark, and wrinkled face. "You are stronger than the lion. He has only his roar. You will be a man after this night," Immopo said. Afterwards Immopo slowly turned from Tingdy and led the other three men away, back to their village. Night was approaching.

Tingdy saw herds of grazing antelopes and they reminded him of cattle he cared for back in his village.

He looked homesick. Tingdy, wearing a rain-soaked red cloth draped over his young, lean body, stood alone holding his spear in his right hand. His stomach felt queasy. His mouth was dry with fear. He had never been alone before in the wild. People here lived by the same laws that governed the wildlife living on the Serengeti, no matter how great or small.

This was his coming of age ceremony. He would have to pass this test to become a man by killing a lion with only his spear and raw courage. If he succeeded, he would be welcomed back into his village a man.

If he failed and lived he would be treated like the village women. He would have to survive alone. Until this day, Tingdy had lived with other boys his same age in a *boma*.

Now fifteen years of age, this was his moment to become a man. This was the traditional way of the Masai. The dark night had arrived!

The rain stung his brown face as he looked sadly in the direction of his village, which was far away. Because of the rain, the red dye was beginning to fade from his skin. Because of the rain, his long orange-colored hair braids were returning to their natural color. Because of the rain, the red cloth that was draped over his right shoulder clung to his lean body. There he stood silently in the cold rain, his presence being revealed by occasional flashes of lightning guarded by Mount Kilimanjaro in the far distance.

Every strange sound that he heard made him flinch. The movement of the tall grass began to look like millions of villagers staring and laughing at him.

A wet blade of grass fell on his bare feet, scaring him. He jumped in fright, thinking it was a snake. Heavy drops of sweat fell from his forehead. He sadly looked in the direction of his village.

Tingdy started humming a song that people back in his village sang to ease his fear.

He squatted down, resting his forehead against his spear. He gripped his spear tighter as he looked down at the cold wet earth beneath his bare feet. The rain began to fall harder.

Later, Tingdy's moments of silence were disturbed when the sounds of hoofbeats and grunts from what sounded like a large animal frantically raced through the thick brush. Tingdy braced himself for whatever was to emerge from the darkness. The unseen beast quickly turned. Tingdy never saw what it was. Frozen with fear, Tingdy could not move. His bare feet were planted to the cold wet floor of the Serengeti and his right hand clenched his spear so firmly that his fingers drew blood from his palm.

After a moment, he could sense something moving in his direction. He could not see. His eyes squinted. Suddenly aided by a bright flash of lightning, he realized he was not alone.

Emerging from the dark was a large, snarling male lion. He had failed to catch the large unseen beast that had startled Tingdy moments before. The lion had found an easier prey.

Frozen with fear, Tingdy dropped his spear. The snarling male lion slowly circled Tingdy.

Flashes of lightning revealed the rain falling from the wooly crown of the King of Beasts. The lion crouched down low to the wet earth, ready to pounce at any moment.

The lion was much larger than Tingdy had ever envisioned. His massive weight could be felt shaking the ground as he slowly walked back and forth summoning his own courage. Then like a flash of lightning the lion bolted into the dark. Moments later, a quite eerie calm fell over the Serengeti.

Tingdy's heart was pounding quickly in his tiny chest like the drums back in his village. He turned slowly looking around for the lion. The lion was gone, but where? The rain had stopped. The cold wind was beginning to blow. Tingdy began to shiver. He got down on the wet ground on his knees and hands searching for his spear.

He found it. He stood erect again and began humming his village song again walking in the dark.

After walking for a while in the dark the glowing eyes of nervous wildebeest quickly vanished as Tingdy startled them while they grazed in the dark. In the distance, he could hear the sound of elephants. He could hear small creeping things on the ground scurrying as he passed. The more Tingdy walked, the more afraid he became.

His skinny brown legs grew tired. He stopped walking and knelt down to rest. His rest was disturbed when the sound of antelope, zebras, and wildebeest grazing ended with sounds of fright that could only mean one thing; there was a danger common to them all lurking in the East African night.

Again coming into view was the large, snarling male lion. He seemed larger and more vicious this time. The lion was aided by the rain that began to fall harder along with the increase of thunder and lightning. Tingdy's eyes grew wide with fear and his breathing quickened as the lion prepared to attack.

Thoughts of running clouded Tingdy's mind. He turned to run and saw visions of his crippled brother; he could hear the village people laughing at him back in the village and he saw himself never being called a man. He sucked in his bottom lip and turned to face the terror of his youth. His time had come. With spear in hand, he confronted the slowly approaching King of Beasts by making quick stabbing jabs.

Having difficulty in seeing the lion at times, he was aided by flashes of lightning as the beast darted to and fro. Each time the lion attacked, Tingdy drove the spear deep into its flesh.

The lion screamed in pain each time he felt Tingdy's spear. The lion at times appeared to bite himself after the sharp spear had pierced his flesh. The massive lion moved quickly into the dark brush. The lion summoned all of his hunting skills to win this battle.

Almost crying, Tingdy laid his spear down and drove his trembling right hand into the wet earth and grabbed a clump of mud. He groaned as he smeared the mud on his wounded left shoulder. His left side was covered with his blood.

Moments passed and the sound of the beast rumbling in the brush returned. After receiving another wound from Tingdy's spear, the lion recovered and moved quickly into the dark. Three times the king of beast made his assault. Tingdy's left shoulder was bleeding from one of the lion's attacks. The pain was so great Tingdy fell to his knees in exhaustion.

Moments passed and the sound of the beast rumbling in the brush returned. Tingdy began to fear the lion was supernatural because he kept attacking again and again, each time more aggressively. The lion leaped one last time. Tingdy rose to his feet and caught a glimpse of the leaping King of Beasts with the aid of a flash of lightning and thrust the spear deep into the lion's chest.

Tingdy fell to the wet earth from exhaustion and the lion crawled into the brush. Later, all was quiet. The only sound was the fading rumble of thunder in the distance and the last sounds of raindrops hitting the wet earth.

Mount Kilimanjaro was coming into view again. The long black night was chased away by a beautiful yellow sunrise.

Immopo and the rest of the tribal leaders returned early in the morning to find an exhausted, shivering Tingdy, and not one, but three dead lions lying scattered in the tall wet Serengeti brush.

Once during the long walk back to his village, an exhausted Tingdy looked back smiling over his right shoulder; he had learned that it was far better to face what confronts you than to run.

Printed in the United States
By Bookmasters